50

ENEAS AFRICANUS

ENEAS AFRICANUS

HARRY STILLWELL EDWARDS

CLASSICS EXPRESS

ENEAS AFRICANUS

A Classics Express Book,
published by Wildside Press, LLC.
www.wildsidebooks.com

WHO HAS THIS CUP?

MAJOR GEORGE E. TOMMEY ADVERTISES FOR HIS SILVER CUP.

Editor *Constitution*, Atlanta, Ga.

Dear Sir: I am writing to invoke your kind assistance in tracing an old family negro of mine who disappeared in 1864, between my stock farm in Floyd County and my home place, locally known as Tommeysville, in Jefferson County. The negro's name was Eneas, a small, grey-haired old fellow and very talkative. The unexpected movement of our army after the battle of Resaca, placed my stock farm in line of the Federal advance and exposed my family to capture. My command, Tommey's Legion, passing within five miles of the place, I was enabled to give them warning, and they hurriedly boarded the last south-bound train. They reached Jefferson County safely but without any baggage, as they did not have time to move a trunk. An effort was made to save the family silver, much of it very old and highly prized, especially a silver cup known in the family as the "Bride's Cup" for some six or eight generations and bearing the inscription:

> *"Ye bryde whose lippes kysse myne*
> *And taste ye water an no wyne*
> *Shall happy live an hersel see*
> *A happy grandchile on each knee."*

These lines were surrounded with a wreath and surmounted by a knight's head, visor down, and the motto: "Semper Fidelis."

This cup was hurriedly packed with other silver in a hair trunk and intrusted to Eneas with verbal instructions as to travel. He drove an old-fashioned, flea-bitten blooded mare to a one-horse wagon full of forage and carried all the Confederate money the family left, to pay his expenses. He was last seen, as I ascertained soon after the war from a wounded member of my command, about eight miles southeast of Atlanta, asleep in the wagon, the mare turning to the right instead of keeping the straight road to Macon. Eneas was a faithful negro, born and raised in the Tommey family and our belief is he was murdered by army stragglers and robbed of the trunk. He had never been over the road he was traveling, as we always traveled to North Georgia by rail, shipping the horses likewise. His geographical knowledge consisted of a few names—places to which I had at different times taken him, and in the neighborhood of my home, such as Macon, Sparta, Louisville, and the counties of Washington and Jefferson. If given a chance to talk he would probably confine himself to "Lady Chain," the mare he was driving; "Lightning," the noted four-mile stallion temporarily in my possession; the Tommey family and our settlement, "Tommeysville." On these topics he could talk eighteen hours a day.

I have no hope of ever seeing Eneas again, for if living he would have gotten back if he had to travel all over the South to do it, but there is a bare chance that the cup may be found, and I am writing to gratify my daughter, whose wedding day is approaching. All brides in the family, since 1670, have used this cup on their wedding days. If the cup was stolen, doubtless the thieves sold it, and if so, the holder may read these lines if they are given publicity. I am willing to waive any question of ownership and purchase the cup at the holder's valuation, if within my power; or, if unwilling to sell, he may loan the cup for a few days.

I shall be greatly obliged if you will publish this letter with a request that all Southern papers, daily and weekly, copy the same. Thanking you in advance and with all good wishes for your happiness and prosperity, I am, most respectfully,

Your obed't servant,

George E. Tommey,
Late Major, Tommey's Legion, C. S. A.
P. O., Louisville, Ga.

* * * *

Althea Lodge, Fayette Co., Ga.
October 15, 1872.

Maj. Geo. E. Tommey,
Louisville, Ga.

Dear Major Tommey: I read with deep interest and sympathy your letter in the *Atlanta Constitution* inquiring of a negro named Eneas. This man, I am sure, came to my house about twenty miles south of Atlanta in 1864. I remember the occasion perfectly, because he mentioned your name and one of my boys was serving in your command. I gave him shelter for the night and food for himself and horse. He insisted on sleeping in his wagon. He told me that the mare was famous on the race track and very valuable and he was afraid to leave her. This struck me as singular, at the time, because she seemed old and broken down. I did not see any trunk, but his wagon was full of hay and fodder and he may have had one hidden under it. Eneas asked me to put him on the road to Thomasville—or so I understood him—and I gave him explicit directions as far as Newnan, advising him to get more at that point. He was gone when I arose next morning. I do hope you will find the old man, as well as the cup. I took quite a fancy to him. He gave me a very vivid description of yourself—whom I had long wished to meet—and of your home, the twelve-room house, lawn with its three fountains, beautiful lake and your hundred negroes in their painted cottages, etc.

Excuse this rambling letter. Your name has stirred an old woman's memories.

Sincerely your friend,
Martha Horton.

P. S.—My son William, who served in your command, married a Connecticut girl. Think of it, Major! But she proved to be a noble-hearted woman and has influenced him to give up tobacco and stimulants in every form. He travels this territory for a New York house. His wife is well connected, and one of her ancestors came over in the Mayflower. She is with me now and sends you her regards. Billy has convinced her that next to General Joseph Johnston, you were the bravest man in the Georgia armies.

M. H.

* * * *

Talbotton, Ga., Oct. 18, 1872.

Major George Tommey, Louisville, Ga.

Sir: Read your letter in the Columbus Enquirer. I kept a livery stable here in '64 and saw the man you are huntin about that time. He drove a broken down old speckled grey mare he called Lady Chain, now that you mention it, and claimed she was in foal to "Lightning," the great four-mile horse. I took this for a joke along with some of the fairy stories he gave me about the Tommeys, but he was so polite and humble that I let him stay over night in the stable. Offered to pay me next morning, an seemed like he had about a bushel of Confedrit money; but I was long on Confed myself and didn't let him put any more on me. Don't remember seein any trunk. He was on his way to Thomasville, so he said, and I giv him as much directions as he could carry.

Very truly,
William Peters.

* * * *

Thomas County, Oct. 19, 1872.

Major George Tommey, Louisville, Ga.

Dear Sir: My wife remembered your old nigger as soon as she read your letter in the paper, and so did I when she called it to my mind. He was a big talker all right, and sat on our back steps half the night talking about the Tommeys, their race horse, twenty-room house, yard with six fountains, and a whole tribe of niggers. We fed him and he slept in his wagon. Next day he wanted to pay me in Confederate money; was using a corn sack for a pocketbook, and it was most full. He moved on to Thomasville, about six miles from here, but I don't think it was the place he was looking for. I reckon it must have been "Tommeysville" he was looking for. Major, I took a good look at Lady Chain and you ain't lost much if you never get her back, but if you don't find the nigger, you've lost the champion liar of Georgia. I hope you get him back, but it's hardly possible a man talking like he did could last seven years on the public road.

Respectfully,

Abner Cummings.

* * * *

Thomasville, Ga., Oct. 19, 1872.

Hon. Sir and Major:

Your man Eneas came to my home in Thomasville in the winter of '65 or the fall of '64, in great distress. He said he had traveled a thousand miles to get to Thomasville, but it wasn't the right Thomasville. He had no idea of States, geography or direction. Claimed he lived in Jefferson County, next to Washington County, and as this describes two counties across the line in Florida, several people at different times had sent him over there. I gave him a letter to a friend over in Jefferson County near Tallahassee. He had an old grey mare he said was a famous race horse, but she didn't look it. Claimed she was in foal to the celebrated "Lightning," whose four-mile race in the mud at New Orleans I witnessed. I thought the old nigger was loose in the upper story. He had no trunk when here.

Very truly,

Andrew Loomis.

* * * *

Tallahassee, Fla., Oct. 20, 1872.

Major Geo. E. Tommey, Tommeysville, via Louisville, Ga.

My Dear Sir: Eneas, your old negro, whose name I had forgotten until I read your letter in a local paper, was on my plantation near here in '65. He came here very blue and utterly discouraged from Thomasville, Ga. Said he was looking for a little Thomasville owned by Major George E. Tommey. He brought a letter from a friend of mine. There are no Tommeys in this county, and no Thomasville, and not knowing what to do with him, I passed him along to Colonel Chairs, a friend in Washington County, which is on the gulf coast. Chairs wrote me that he had had a great deal of fun out of Eneas. The gulf astonished him. He declared solemnly that he knew he was in the wrong Washington, because there were no oranges, or scrub palmettoes, or big green spiders (crabs) in his, and the water had no salt in it. Eneas talked a good deal of Macon and Louisville, and there being a county and town so named, besides another Thomasville, to the north in Alabama, Chairs started him up that way. I am truly sorry the old man came to grief. He was a harmless old fellow, though a picturesque liar, as are many old negroes when they talk of their white folks.

It is possible that Eneas had a trunk, but I have no recollection of seeing one in his possession.

Yours very truly,

Randolph Thomas.

* * * *

Louisville, Ala., Oct. 28, 1872.

Major Tommey, Louisville, Ga.

Sir: A ole nigger name of enus come by hyar in the firs yer atter the war with er old mare an er colt he claim was by the lightnin. He was lokin for a tomusville, an I tried to show him the way back to tomusville, in Georgia, but he got mad and wanted to fight me, an ef he hadnt ben er ole man I would have busted him open. Mr. tommy, you wont never see yo nigger no more less he mends his way of acktin when you are tryin to help him.

Respectfull, sir, yours,

Pompey Wiley (Colored).

He lef hyar for Macon County.

* * * *

Barton, Washington County, Ala.

Major G. E. Tommey, Louisville, Ga.

Dear Sir: Your negro, Eneas, came to my place in this county in 1865, I think, from a little village named Thomasville to the northeast. He was very poor and his pathetic story appealed to my sympathies. I let him have some rations and a piece of land and he planted a cotton crop. He married a young mulatto woman on my place that year, and when he left here about Christmas, 1866, carried with him a young baby besides the old mare and her colt. The colt, by the way, was a beauty.

Eneas was a puzzle to me, though I have lived among negroes all my life. His stories of you and your place were marvels. But for the fact that he held the mare and colt in your name, refusing dozens of offers for the latter when in dire need, I should have put him down a reckless romancer. He began preaching here among the negroes and proved to be a most eloquent spiritual advocate. He claimed to be the pastor of a big congregation at home. I heard him on one occasion when he baptized forty converts and was thrilled by his imagery and power.

Eneas knew nothing of geography beyond the names of a few towns and counties. Hearing of a Macon and Louisville over in Mississippi, he gathered his household goods into his wagon in December, '66. I do hope you will yet find him. Suppose you make inquiries through the African Methodist Church? He ought to be a bishop by this time.

Very respectfully,
James Tally,
Attorney at Law.

* * * *

Sunshine Parsonage,
Washington County, Mississippi.

Major Geo. E. Tommey, Louisville, Ga.

My Dear Sir: I was greatly interested in your letter copied into our county paper from the *Atlanta Constitution*, concerning

Eneas Tommey. He was here in 1868 or 1869 with a wife and several children. They came in a one-horse wagon drawn by an old grey mare he called Lady Chain, and followed by a splendid young colt he declared was from celebrated racing stock. An almost worn out pass from his mistress, Mrs. Tommey, though it bore no date or address, saved the old man from arrest. His story, that he was lost and on his way home, though remarkable, was possible, and he was not molested. The narrative of his wanderings interested me greatly. He came up the river—the Mississippi—from Jefferson County, trying to find a ford. He had heard of a Washington parish and a Thomasville in Louisiana, and was trying to reach them. He rented a piece of land near here and raised a crop, leaving in 1869 for Jefferson County, Alabama. I gave him a letter to a minister in that county.

Very truly,

(Rev.) John Simms.

P. S.—I regret to say that after leaving here, Eneas, though an active minister of the Gospel, suffered the young horse to be entered in a county race. I understand that he won about $75. Allowance, however, must be made for the old man's necessities and distress.

J. S.

* * * *

Idlewilde, Jefferson County, Ala.
October 26, 1872.

Major Geo. E. Tommey, Louisville, Ga.

My Dear Sir: A Birmingham paper to-day gave me the explanation of a mystery that has puzzled my family for several years, when it reproduced your letter to the *Atlanta Constitution.* Eneas—or the Rev. Eneas Tommey, as he called himself—

came here in 1869 with a grey mare, and a splendid young horse, which he claimed was of marvelous speed, and a letter from a friend of mine in Mississippi. He also brought a wife and two children. To the latter he added a third before leaving. My daughter was greatly interested in the old man's remarkable story, and made an effort to help him. She took down a letter to you, which he dictated, made seven copies of it and sent one to every Thomasville in the South. They all came back to her. By good luck she retained one for her scrapbook, and I enclose it that you may see how the faithful old fellow was trying to reach you. He stayed around here farming and preaching until 1870 when, hearing from a horse trader of a Macon and a Sparta in Tennessee, he moved on. He had no trunk with him, and I am afraid your cup is gone.

Very truly,

(Rev.) Amos Wells.

P. S.—I am informed that Eneas participated in a horse race in Birmingham after leaving here, and won a great deal of money.

A. W.

* * * *

Letter of Eneas inclosed in that of Rev. Mr. Wells:

Marse George: I am loss in er distric called Yellerhama, by a town name o'Burningham. Ef you knows whar Burningham is, fer God's sake come ter me fer I can't git ter you! Me an' Lady Chain is plum wore out.

Marse George, I been ter firs one an' den ernuther Thomasville, year in an' year out, tell thar ain't no sense in hit. An' I ain't hit de right one yit. Evy yuther place is name Thomasville er Macon er Washington er Jefferson. Evybody knows whar I wanter go but me, an' shows me de road; but all I kin do is ter keep er movin'. De firs Thomasville I got ter I got back fo' times. Hit was harder ter lose it than hit was ter find it!

Marse George, I come ter one pond I couldn't see ercross an' de water warn't no count. The last Thomasville was out most ter sundown an' I was headin' fer ernuther when I struck er creek er mile wide an' Lady Chain couldn't wade hit, so we turn back.

Marse George, Lady Chain's colt come, back in the secon' Jefferson, an' he sholy is ole Lightnin's colt; long-legged, big-footed an' iron grey. I been tryin' him out hyar an' thar an' thar ain't nothin' kin tech him.

Marse George, I got ernuther wife down in de third Washington an' am bringin' her erlong. She weighs one hundred and sixty, an' picks fo' hundred pounds er cotton er day. She b'longs ter you, same as me an' Lady Chain an' de colt.

Marse George, er horse trader goin' by told me erbout some more Macons an' Spartas an' Jeffersons an' Washingtons up de country fum hyar an' ef I don't git word fum you by nex' month, I'm gointer move erlong.

Marse George, ef you knows whar I is fum dis hyar letter an' can't come yo'self, sen' fer me. I'm sick o' de road an' wanter git home. Do somp'n an' do it quick!

Yo' ole nigger,

Eneas.

* * * *

Macon, Tenn., Oct. 30, 1872.

Maj. George E. Tommey, Louisville, Ga.

My Dear Sir: Eneas was here in 1869 or 1870 and remained about a year preaching at Mt. Zion and other places in the county. I do not know when I ever met a more original and entertaining talker. His description of your colonial house with its forty rooms, white columns and splendid parks has aroused in me a strong desire to visit the place if I am ever able to come to Georgia. I know it must have suffered from the ravages of the war, but doubtless enough remains to show its former magnificence. I am especially anxious to see the great lake with its flock of swans, and the twelve fountains on your lawn. My mother is a Georgian and have often heard her describe the natural beauties of the State. There is a feeling with us all that at last it is "home" and that some day we shall all assemble in dear old Monroe county where grandpa was born.

Eneas brought with him to this place a grey mare that was, he said, a famous race horse, and that the father of her colt was the greatest horse in the world. I had forgotten their names until I read your letter. Eneas insisted that you lived at Thomasville next to Washington and Jefferson Counties, and near a town named Louisville. There are towns and counties of the same names in this State and he left to visit them. He seemed to have plenty of money. I hope you will hear from him yet, but I am afraid the trunk is gone. He had none when here.

Sincerely yours,

Mary Adkins.

* * * *

Louisville, Tenn., Oct. 27, 1872.

Sir: Don't you worry about old Eneas. He came here in or about '70 with a grey mare, a long-legged race horse, a young wife and three children, and give out that he was a minister of the Gospel. They stayed on my place and there were four children when they left. He was a preacher all right, cause I heard him time and again, but all the same he was the biggest liar in Tennessee at that time, and that's a great record for any man. Major, if half he said about you and your place is true, you ought to be President. You must have owned all the niggers in Georgia, and your home must be spread over all three of them counties he has been looking for ever since freedom. About that Lightning colt—he certainly looks it. Eneas slipped him into a free-for-all up here and him and a strange white man about busted the county. I offered him $500 for the colt, but he said your price was $20,000. Considering you had never seen him, I thought that a little high and him and me didn't trade. Next day he was gone. Oh, you Eneas! Say, Major, if he ever gets back, and he will, for you can't lose that kind of man for good, better nail down everything movable—including them twelve fountains.

Yours,

Tom Johnson.

P. S.—I say; twelve fountains!
P. S. S.—Forty-four rooms! Gosh! is the Legion still with you?

* * * *

Washington County, N. C., Oct. 20, 1872.

Maj. George E. Tommey, Louisville, Ga.

My Dear Major: Your old negro has been on my plantation for about a year farming and preaching and romancing. He came straight through Tennessee and North Carolina, touching Sparta, Louisville, Washington and Jefferson Counties in the former, and the towns of Jefferson, Sparta and Macon in this State before he found me. I am affectionately known all over this section of the State as "Major Tommy," and as the old negro was looking for "Major Tommey," somebody put him on my trail. He soon had me treed, but was greatly disappointed when he saw me. However, that did not keep him from paying me a year's visit. Eneas is a queer character—wisdom of the serpent and simplicity of a child. His story, probably growing with age like the stories of some of our veterans, has beguiled many a lonely hour for me, but not until I read your letter in the *Richmond Dispatch* did I give him credit for many facts in it. The young race horse is certainly a fine animal and should you decide to sell him I trust you will give me the refusal. Eneas won several purses up here in local races. It seems he has a new name for his horse everywhere he goes. He says it keeps him from getting "too common." When Eneas was not plowing or racing, his favorite occupation was preaching, his subject usually being the wandering of the Hebrews in the desert. He left here for Jefferson, S. C. I am sorry to say, I heard no mention of your lost cup, and if he had any trunk I was not informed of it.

With regards for yourself and all good wishes for the young bride, I am,

Very sincerely yours,
Thomas Bailey,
(Late) Major 13th N. C.
Volunteers, C.S.A.

* * * *

Extract from Columbia (S. C.) Register, October 27, 1872:

One of the surprises of yesterday's races came in the free-for-all two-mile dash, which was won by "Chainlightning," entered by an old negro man calling himself Eneas Tommey, who claims the horse was sired by the celebrated stallion Lightning, and that the dam, which he drives to a one-horse wagon on his way to Georgia, is "Lady Chain." She was certainly a tired looking old lady. Eneas arrived late and at once attracted attention by his unique appearance and his limitless faith in Chainlightning. His story and the splendid horse interested some stablemen and after a private demonstration they succeeded in getting him entered and a rider engaged. In the get-off Chainlightning took the lead and gave a marvelous exhibition of speed. He led the bunch by a hundred yards at the end of the first mile and by nearly three hundred at the end of the second. He was then going strong and the efforts of the rider to stop him resulted in a runaway. When he came around the third time the crowd blocked the track and brought him to a standstill, but his rider was thrown. Eneas won $200. It is not known how his backers fared, but it is supposed that they cleaned up a good pile on the side. Eneas left on yesterday, going toward Augusta, Ga. It was suggested afterwards that this may have been the man advertised for in the *Atlanta Constitution* by a Major Tommey, of Louisville, Ga., a few weeks ago. The matter will be brought to his attention. One reason for the sudden departure of the old negro, who had become quite a hero among members of his race, is said to be a movement to elect him to the State Senate.

* * * *

Louisville, Ga.—(Correspondence *Macon Telegraph and Messenger*, Oct. 31, '72.)—Your correspondent on Thursday last was the favored guest of Major George E. Tommey, the famous commander of the Tommey Legion, which rendered conspicuous service to the Confederacy as part of Johnston's—afterwards Hood's—army, in the Tennessee and North Georgia campaigns. The Major lives about twelve miles from this place at Tommeysville, as his plantation is called. His delightful residence is one of the old-fashioned two-story houses with broad hall and verandahs and two large wings, and is situated in a beautiful grove of oak and hickory. The broad lawn in front abounds with roses and among them is a tiny fountain with a spray. Beyond the house lie the barns and the negro quarters and a small artificial lake where ducks abound. Sherman's army missed the charming spot and the only suggestion of the late unpleasantness is the Major's sword crossed with the colors of the Legion over the broad fireplace at the end of the hall.

The occasion of your correspondent's visit was the marriage of the Major's only daughter, Beauregarde Forrest, to Mirabeau Lamar Temple, of Dallas, Texas. The bride, a petite brunette of great beauty, entered life eighteen years ago, inheriting her mother's name, but by the act of the Georgia Legislature this was changed in honor of the two heroes of the Confederacy dear to the heart of her illustrious father. The groom bears the name of two Georgia families long ago transplated to the Lone Star State and is an attorney of great promise.

The wedding supper was charming in its simplicity and homeliness, using the word in its original sense. The broad back porch between the two wings was closed in with smilax and the feast was spread on a great home-made table twenty feet in diameter. Seats were placed for forty. Such a display of delicacies and substantials has not been seen in this section since the good old days before the war. The low growing ferns and cut-flowers of the decorations—there by the hundreds—did not hide the guests' smiling faces. Wine, the famous scuppernong of the Major's own vintage, was the only stimulant visible, for the Major and his good lady are almost total abstainers. When the guests were seated a grace was pronounced by the Rev. Mr. Thigpen, and fun and merriment broke loose. Toast after toast was given and sentiment and the poets were interspersed with songs from the family negroes assembled in the backyard by a gigantic bonfire. Some of the songs were of exquisite harmony and pathos. Freedom, so far, had brought but little of brightness into the lives of these humble people.

A dramatic situation that will one day enter into a story, came during the supper festivities. A sudden excitement among the negroes was followed by cries, some of merriment and some of fear, and by a stampede of the juniors. In the red light of the bonfire an old negro suddenly appeared, reining up a splendid grey horse. The old man was seated in a red-wheeled road cart, enveloped in a flopping linen duster, and wore a silk hat. His "Whoa, Chainlightning!" resounded all over the place. Then he stood up and began to shout about Moses and the Hebrew children being led out of Egypt into the promised land. Major Tommey listened for a brief instant and rushed out. The newcomer met him with an equal rush and their loud greetings floated back to us clear as the notes of a plantation bell: "Eneas, you black rascal, where have you been?"

"O! Lord, Marse George! Glory be ter God! Out o' de wilderness! De projeckin' son am back ergin!"

"It's Eneas!" screamed the little bride, gathering up her skirts and rushing out. In the strong light, as the wedding party hurriedly followed, we could see the old negro hanging to his master as he filled the night with his weird cries. Catching the excitement, the negroes around began to moan and chant, taking their text from the old man's words.

"Where have you been, sir?" The Major was trying to free himself and choking with tears and laughter.

"All over de blessed worl', Marse George! But I'm home ergin!—You hyar me, niggers?—home ergin!"

"Stop, sir!"—But suddenly the old man grew rigid in the grasp of a momentous thought. His voice sank to a whisper audible to only a few of us:

"Marse George, wha's Nancy?"

"Nancy is dead, Eneas," said the Major, sadly.

"Thank God!" said the old man fervently.

"Where is my trunk, Eneas?" The old negro was making a horn of his hands and giving the plantation halloo. With his eyes set on the banking shadows beyond the fire, he waited, an inscrutable smile on his wrinkled face. Presently, into the circle of light came an old grey mare, drawing a wagon in which sat a yellow woman, hovering a small colony of children.

"I done brought you a whole bunch o' new Yellerhama, Burningham niggers, Marse George! Some folks tell me dey is free, but I know dey b'long ter Marse George Tommey des like Lady Chain and her colt! Marse George, you oughter see dat horse—"

"Where is the trunk?" repeated the Major, laughing and wiping his eyes. "Where did you leave it, Eneas?"

"I ain't left hit," said Eneas, indignantly. "Git out o' dat wagon, niggers, fo' I bus somer you wide open!" The little colony fell over the wheels like cooters from a log, and drawing aside the hay that had held them, Eneas brought forth a time and weather defying hair trunk. He heaved a mighty sigh of relief as he dropped it on the ground:

"Dar 'tis, Marse George, an' I sho is glad to git shut o' dat ol' bunch o' hide an' hair!" The bride danced and clapped her tiny hands: "My cup! My cup! Get it! Quick! O, please somebody open the trunk!"

Major Tommey picked up an axe and with one blow sliced off the ancient lock. From its snug nest in cotton batting, the bride lifted a shining cup, the cup, Mr. Editor, advertised in your columns a few weeks ago. A bucket rattled down in the nearby well and the bride-groom came with a great gourd to fill it. Then he read aloud the quaint inscription:

"Ye bryde whose lippes kysse myne
An taste ye water an no wyne
Shall happy live and hersel see
A happy grandchile on each knee."

The little woman accepted the challenge with the cup, and smiling up to the face of her husband sipped of the crystal draught and handed him the cup. He, too, drank, but the slight flush on the bride's face was as nothing to the fiery scarlet of his own when a storm of applause greeted the act.

Eneas had drawn the Major aside and produced an old strap pocketbook stuffed with bills.

"Marse George," he began, "de bag o' yaller war money what dey gimme warn't no good over yonner whar I been. Countin' de c'llections I tuck up in the church an' what I winned on de track wid Chainlightnin' an' ain't spent—"

"Keep it, Eneas," said the Major, almost exploding with laughter, and patting the old man on the shoulder, "that bunch of Burningham Yellerhama niggers more than squares us!"

68663533R20017

Made in the USA
Columbia, SC
09 August 2019